For IXV

Published by Roaring Brook Press • Roaring Brook Press is a division of Holtzbrinck Publishing Holdings Limited Partnership
120 Broadway, New York, NY 10271 • mackids.com • Copyright © 2021 by Elisha Cooper • All rights reserved.

Library of Congress Control Number 2020907356 • ISBN 978-1-250-25733-8

Our books may be purchased in bulk for promotional, educational, or business use. Please contact your local bookseller or the Macmillan
Corporate and Premium Sales Department at (800) 221-7945 ext. 5442 or by email at MacmillanSpecialMarkets@macmillan.com.

First edition, 2021 • Book design by Elizabeth Clark and Elisha Cooper • The illustrations for this book were created with ink and watercolor.
Printed in China by Toppan Leefung Printing Ltd., Dongguan City, Guangdong Province

1 3 5 7 9 10 8 6 4 2

yes
&
no

elisha cooper

ROARING BROOK PRESS • NEW YORK

Good morning, good morning!

It's time to wake up.

Are you both excited for the day?

Yes, I *am* excited.

Hmpff

Now, would you like something to eat?

Yes, I would! I would like to eat something very much.

No. I already ate.

Can we all clean up a little?

Yes!

Never.

And now, as the work of the day begins,
can you two play with each other?

Yes, we can!

No, thank you.

No.

No.

No, no.

Nope.

Hmmm . . .
It's a beautiful day.
Maybe you two can play
outside?

Yes.

Yes.

Yes.

Yes.

Yes.

Well, if I must.

Yes.

Yes.

Oh! I see you caught your tail.

That's nice, but . . .

ENOUGH!

What. Are. You. Doing?
You have got to find another
way to spend your day.
Both of you. Go!

And look out for each other.

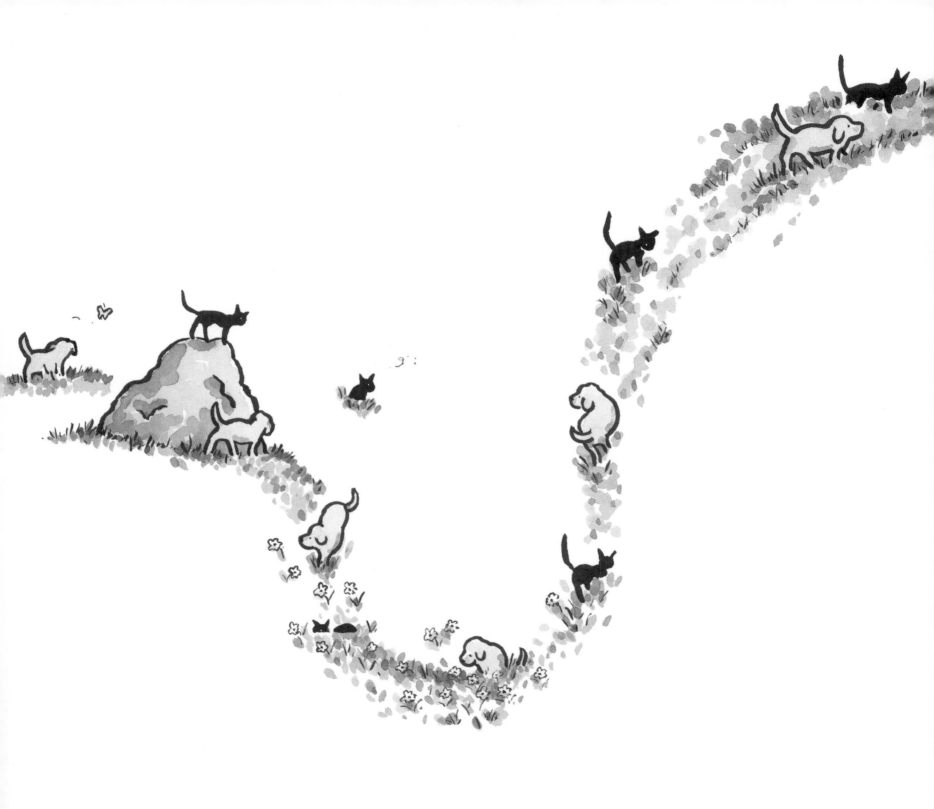

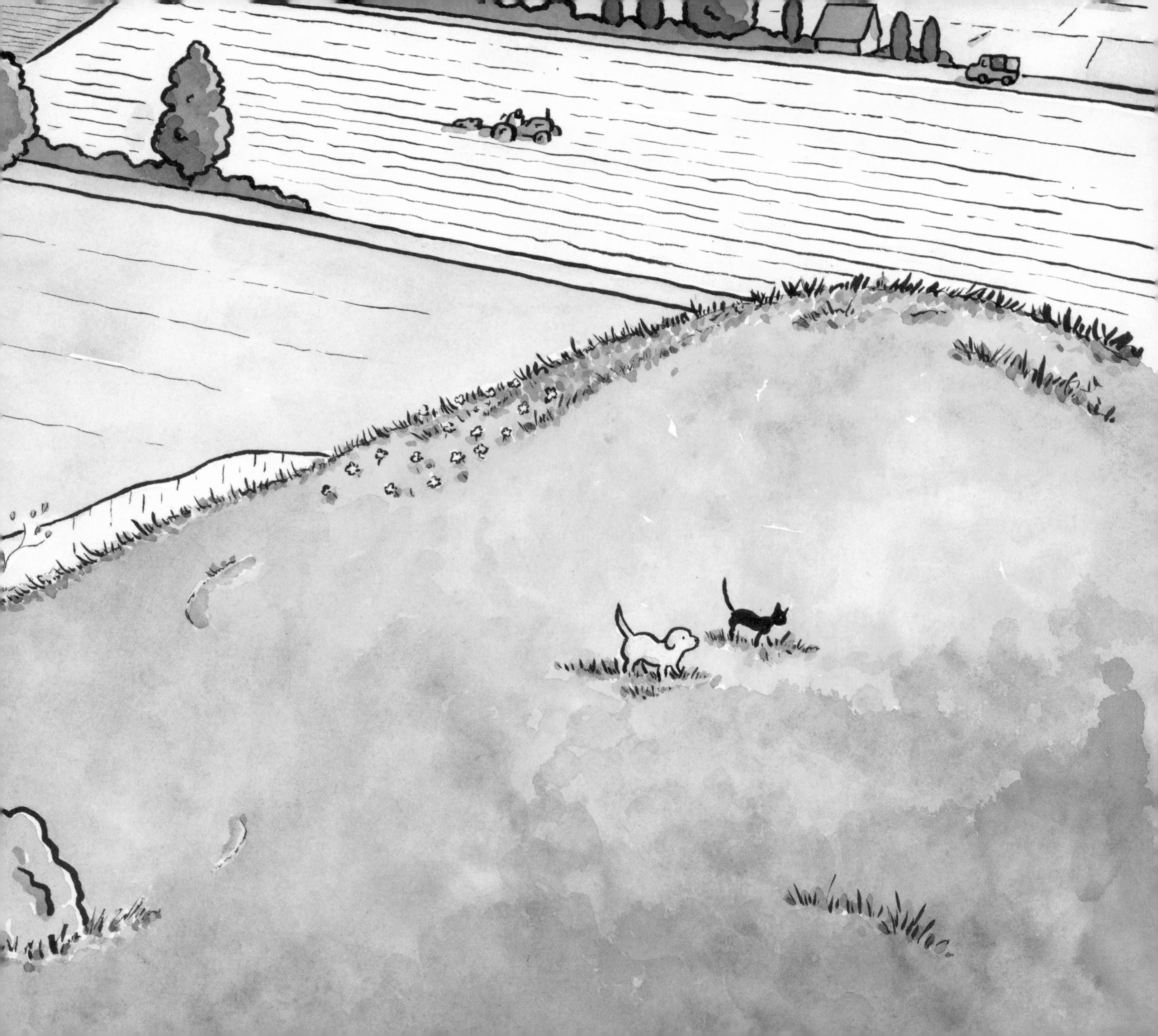

Yes.

Good night, good night.
Are you ready to sleep?

And we are here and you are here
and that will always be so.

I know.

Can you think of all the good things today?

I guess.

And you know you can do all those things again tomorrow.

I suppose.

And get ready for bed?

No, not yet.

My dear. Did you have a good day?

Yes and no.
The day was good
but now it's done.

Now, would you like something to eat?

Well, okay...

Can we all clean up a little?

Hffllmmmp

It is time.

No.

No.

No.

No.

No.

Hello out there! It's time to come in.

It's time to come inside.

Nooooo.